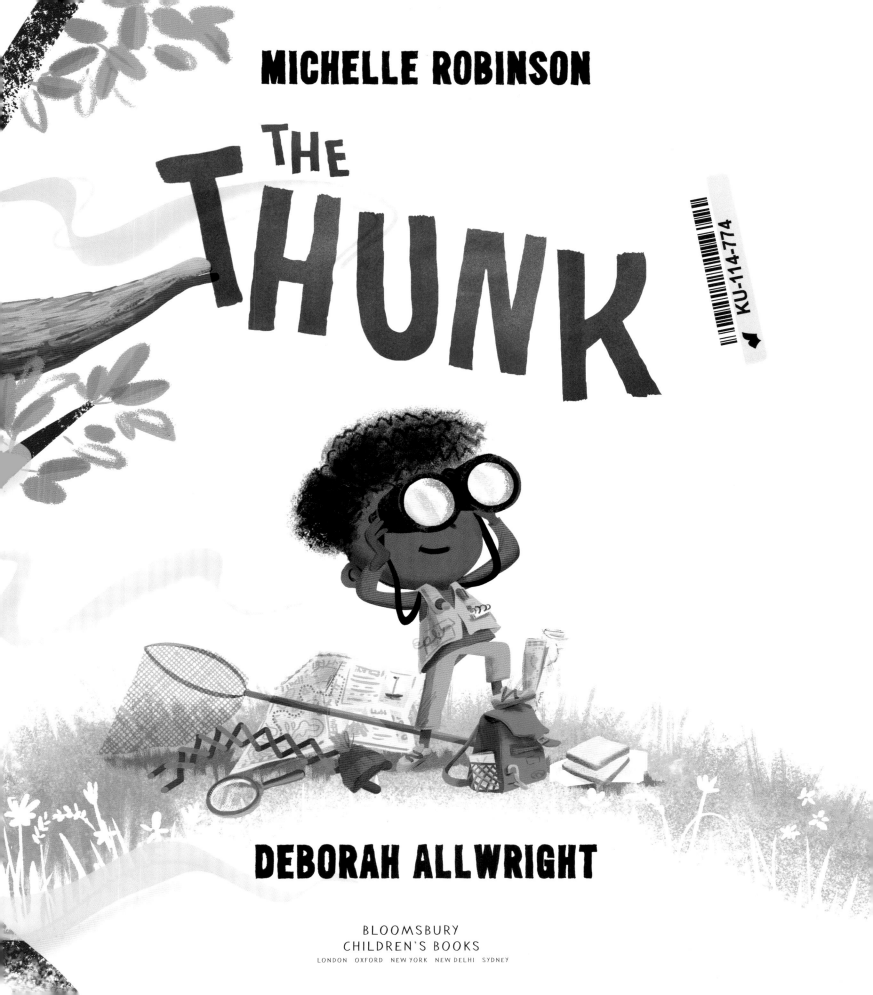

MICHELLE ROBINSON

THE THUNK

DEBORAH ALLWRIGHT

BLOOMSBURY
CHILDREN'S BOOKS

LONDON OXFORD NEW YORK NEW DELHI SYDNEY

Have you heard of the **Thunk?**

It's a bit like a **skink,**

although more like a **skunk** on account of the stink.

and its fur's
blue-ish pink

and it's ever-so-slightly
completely . . .

The Thunk
has a trunk

... **EXTINCT.**

Some say, "That's not TRUE.

Thunks have **NEVER** existed.

They're just an old legend

that grew and got twisted.

But there is **one person** who's always insisted
that he'll find a Thunk, on his own, unassisted.

Meet **Hector Voltaire.**
Hector's had his fair share
of other kids saying his head's full of air.

They tease and they taunt him.
He tries not to care.

"I'm sure there are ALL SORTS of WONDERS out there."

"The cave of a dragon.

A hobgoblin's hole.

A lake with a monster.

A bridge with a troll.

A rare fairy toadstool.

A unicorn foal.

But . . .

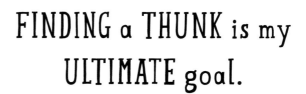

FINDING a THUNK is my
ULTIMATE goal.

If those kids are all wrong
and I'm right . . . what a thrill!"
But finding a Thunk will take
patience and skill . . .

. . . and teabags

and toast forks,

a tent and
some pegs.

Some bread and
some butter,

a few
dozen eggs,

plus root beer
(in barrels),

and ketchup
(in kegs),

and one of those
chairs that stands
up on three legs.

Hector's not NORMALLY brave,
strong or strapping.

But look at him go!

He's not flustered or flapping.

"If only," he thinks, "I were better at mapping . . ."

He's lost!

But he's found . . .

... where some creature's been napping!

Here are some bluebells
picked fresh from the dell.

And there is a teacup –
a saucer as well.

Some paw prints,
some fur . . .

Bluish-pink?

Hard to tell.

And a truly,
stupendously. . .

...TERRIBLE smell!

Meanwhile, the rarest of beasts in the land
is taking his afternoon stroll, just as planned.
(His mouldy old odour, you must understand,
needs a lot of fresh air lest it get out of hand.)

Having wafted his uncommon fragrance about

the Thunk raises up his magnificent snout,

sniffs the air and concludes,

"It is good to be out."

But the peace is disturbed
by a jubilant shout.

"YAHOOEY!
I knew it!
You ARE real!
High five!
I'll be famous for finding
the LAST THUNK alive!

But is there just
one of you . . . ?"

The Thunks THRIVE!

Hector counts TWO of them.

"Three, four and FIVE."

The Thunks gather round him.
He counts quite a few.

"Sixty three thousand, four hundred and two."

They'll **have** to believe me. They'll see that it's true!

BUT . . .

what if they put all the

Thunks

in a ZOO?"

The thought makes him sad. "I'm not totally sure that I still want to prove you exist anymore.

And I certainly wasn't **this** happy before — can I stay here with you?"

The Thunk opens his door.

What a rare, happy creature is Hector Voltaire!
With no one to tease him and never a care.
And the windows thrown open to freshen the air —
there's a WORLD of adventures to seek out and share!

With teabags

and toast forks,

and freshly-baked
rolls . . .

... with fairies, with unicorns,

monsters and trolls.

Each night he beds down in his cosy top bunk
with a dream, and a map . . .

...and his **best friend**, the Thunk.